SPECIAL DELIVERY

Joe Austen

CARLTON UK
Television

sapling

First published in 1996 by Sapling, an imprint of Boxtree
Ltd, Broadwall House, 21 Broadwall, London SE1 9PL

The Story Store is a Yesterland/TVC production for
Carlton UK Television.

10 9 8 7 6 5 4 3 2 1

Photographs by Peter Ellmore and Simon Paul
Puppets posed by Martin Pullen
Cover designed by Tracey Cunnell
Designed by Dan Newman
Reproduction by SX Composing DTP
Printed and bound in Great Britain by Cambus Litho Ltd

ISBN: 0 7522 0169 7

A CIP catalogue entry for this book is available from the
British Library

THE STORY STORE

The Story Store is the most wonderful shop in the world.
It sells Vanishing Cream, Shrinking Powder, Move-O
Machines, Flying Umbrellas, Speed-O Powder, Tap Dancers,
Sausage Trees, Helping Hands, and an endless variety of
magical goods of every description.
George runs The Story Store with the assistance of Pip, his
best friend in all the world.
Every time the doors of The Story Store are opened,
something amazing is sure to happen...

One fine day, George was in The Story Store arranging a display of boxes, when Pip came running in, playing with his friend the Dog Biscuit.

Pip crashed into the boxes.

George picked Pip up and set him on his feet.

"Off you go, Pip," he said. "And don't get into any more mischief."

Sammy Clump arrived with a note from his Granny.

"Here's what your Granny wants," said George. "A packet of Vanish-O washing powder, and a packet of Raise-O flour."

Pip and the Dog Biscuit tried to rebuild George's display.

But Pip fell into the boxes with another loud crash.

To keep Pip out of mischief, George sent him to Granny Clump's house with the washing powder and flour.

"And don't get them mixed up," George warned, as he began to rebuild the display.

But as Pip and the Dog Biscuit played in the street, they dropped the packets in a puddle.

Granny couldn't tell one muddy packet from the other.

When Pip told her which was the packet of flour, she baked her cakes with it.

Then she washed her petticoats with the washing powder.

"Mmmm. Those cakes smell delicious," she said.
But suddenly she began to float in the air.
"Get me down!" she screamed. "Help!"

Pip was amazed to see the cakes disappear one by one.

"Go and fetch George to get me down from here," Granny cried. "Hurry, Pip. Hurry!"

So Pip ran back to The Story Store as fast as his legs would carry him.

George and Sammy had almost rebuilt the display of boxes when Pip rushed in and knocked them down with a crash.

Pip squeaked excitedly to George and Sammy, who followed him back to Granny's garden.

George realized that Pip had mixed up the boxes, and that Granny had washed her petticoats in the self-raising flour – which is why she was floating in the air!

And the Vanish-O powder in the cakes had made them all disappear!

As George and Sammy waited for Granny to take off her floating petticoats, Pip hid behind a bush.

"I blame Pip for this mix-up," George told Sammy. "Sometimes I think I'd be better off without him altogether."

When Pip heard those words, a tear rolled down his cheek.

17

He knew what he must do.

He would go far, far away where nobody would ever find him. And never be any trouble to George, or anyone else, ever again.

He said goodbye to his friend the Dog Biscuit.
And then he set off into the lonely wilderness.

In Granny's garden, George didn't know that Pip was gone.

"But you know, Sammy," he said. "Pip is my best friend in all the world. I don't know what I'd do without him."

Pip struggled through the howling wind alone. All alone.

When George discovered that Pip had gone away, he was
heartbroken.

As night fell, he set off in the dark and the storm to find Pip.

Far, far away, Pip huddled in the shelter of a tree as the raging
storm howled around him.

"Pip! Pip!" George shouted. "Come back to me Pip! It's George."

The Dog Biscuit heard George's voice, and ran up to him, barking eagerly.

The Dog Biscuit was able to follow Pip's scent in the dark, and soon led George to where a lonely Pip was trying to take shelter from the storm.

The light of George's lantern fell upon Pip's face.

Squeaking with delight, Pip ran towards George.

He leapt into his arms.

"We found you, Pip. We found you at last!" George laughed.

In The Story Store, Granny Clump had found a box of real Raise-O flour and had made some cakes, while Sammy rebuilt George's display of boxes.

The smell of the cakes led the Dog Biscuit through the dark night back to the warmth and comfort of The Story Store.

Granny and Sammy were overjoyed to see George and Pip safe and sound once more.

They decided to celebrate by having Granny Clump's delicious cakes, and to show Pip how much they loved him, he was allowed to have the first cake.

But just as he was about to pick it up, the cake rose into the air and
flew away,

"Oh dear," said Granny. "I must have used too much Raise-O flour in
that one."

30

"Squeak! Squeak! Squeak!" said Pip as he ran after the cake. And then he crashed into the boxes.

"I don't believe it," said George.
"He's done it again!"
And this time, they all laughed.

THE END